MAGGIE SPARKS

AND THE

TRUTH DRAGON

STEVE SMALLMAN

ILLUSTRATED BY
ESTHER HERNANDO

MAGGIE
That's me!

BAT
The coolest chameleon EVER.

MUM
Super smart. Bakes great cookies.

DAD
Writes a lot. Cannot bake cookies.

AUNT CELIA
Posh. Likes weird food.

Published by Sweet Cherry Publishing Limited
Unit 36, Vulcan House,
Vulcan Road,
Leicester, LE5 3EF
United Kingdom

First published in the UK in 2022
2022 edition

2 4 6 8 10 9 7 5 3 1

ISBN: 978-1-78226-715-7

Maggie Sparks and the Truth Dragon

Cover design by Esther Hernando and Brandon Mattless
Illustrations by Esther Hernando

www.sweetcherrypublishing.com

Printed and bound in Turkey

ALFIE
Stinky and
annoying.

GRANDAD
My favourite
wizard in the world!

UNCLE
ROGER
Always on
his phone.

ELLA
World's worst cousin!

ARTHUR
My best friend.

CHAPTER 1

Maggie Sparks was a witch. A small, curly-haired, freckle-faced witch, who was usually full of mischief and fizzing with

MAGIC.

But today she wasn't *just* a witch …

she was a fashion queen!

She was dressed to impress in stripy leggings, a rainbow T-shirt, a tutu, spotty wellies, a black leather jacket and her superstar sunglasses. Bat, her pet chameleon, was VERY impressed. He gave her a thumbs up with all four of his thumbs!

Maggie hurried downstairs
to show her mum and dad how
awesome she looked.

'Ta-da!' she said, as she struck a
pose in the living room doorway.

Mum and Dad looked VERY
surprised, and very smart.

'Why do you both look so posh?'
asked Maggie.

'Because we're all going to Aunt
Celia and Uncle Roger's for dinner,'
said Mum. 'You can't go dressed like
that. Wear this instead.'

Mum handed Maggie a boring
navy-blue dress and the smart shiny
shoes that pinched her toes.

Maggie's face fell into a frown. 'What?! This is SOOOO UNFAIR!' she shouted. Then she stomped back upstairs to get changed.

The journey to Aunt Celia's house was awful. The car was hot and stuffy, and Alfie wouldn't stop screaming until Mum gave him a biscuit. Then he covered himself and everyone else in crumbs and biscuity slobber.

By the time Maggie's family arrived at The Fanshaw Residence (that's what Aunt Celia called her house),

they were all red-faced, crumpled
and smeared with custard creams.

'Tom, Hetty, you made it … at last!' said Aunt Celia, opening the giant front door.

'Yes,' said Mum. 'Sorry we're a bit late, the traffic was–'

'It doesn't matter, Hetty, dear,' Aunt Celia interrupted. 'I'm sure you did your best. And I'm so glad you didn't

bother to dress up. We're not fussy!'

Mum forced her face into a smile and Dad rolled his eyes.

As they stepped inside, Aunt Celia said, 'Shoes off, please. We've got a new carpet in the living room.'

Maggie happily kicked off her smart shoes, forgetting that the sock on her right foot had a big hole in it. One toe peeped out and wiggled like a worm.

Mum blushed as Aunt Celia tutted.

'Bring your shoes with you,' said Aunt Celia. 'I think it will be best if we eat outside, on the patio.' She looked at Alfie and added, 'Less mess!'

They walked through the hall, waded through the thick, new, living room carpet and stepped out onto the patio. Uncle Roger was lounging in a garden chair, talking into his mobile phone. He looked up and waved, then turned back and carried on with his call.

'He'll be with us soon,' said Aunt Celia. 'It's an important business call from America. He works so hard.'

Does he? thought Maggie. She didn't think talking on the phone counted as hard work. Maths homework, on the other hand – now THAT was hard work.

Just then, Maggie's cousin Ella came running towards them. She looked perfect, as usual. Ella had beautiful curly hair, brown eyes and white teeth. She was dressed in clothes that made her look cool and smart and sporty all at the same time. She was SOOOOOO annoying!

'Hello, Auntie Hetty and Uncle Tom,' said Ella. 'Wow, you both look lovely!'

Mum smiled. Dad blushed and said, 'Thanks, Ella.'

'And hello, Maggie,' Ella said, turning to face her.

'What an unusual pattern on your dress!'

Maggie looked down and saw two biscuity Alfie handprints.

Ella laughed.

Maggie didn't.

Dinner was awful! There was lots of weird-looking food and no chips. Worst of all, Aunt Celia droned on and on about all the lovely things she'd bought since their last visit, and how well Ella was getting on at school.

Maggie was SO BORED!
So when Mum said, 'Ella, why don't
you show Maggie around your lovely
garden?' Maggie was happy to leave
the table.

'Let's play Tap-it Tennis!' said Ella.

'Tip-tap – what?' said Maggie.

Ella giggled. 'It's just like normal tennis. But the ball is attached to a pole with string, so you can't hit it into next door's garden by mistake.'

Maggie sighed. Hitting the ball into next door's garden was her favourite thing about tennis. Especially when it slam-dunked into their pond!

Ella handed Maggie a racket and then hit the ball gently with hers. The ball swung round on the rope and Maggie hit it back.

Well, this isn't too bad, Maggie thought, as she and Ella tapped the ball back and forth.

But after a few minutes, Ella started to hit the ball harder and harder. Maggie could hardly keep up! The ball was whizzing past her eyes like a streak of fuzzy yellow lightning.

Then Ella hit the ball so hard it made a THUNK! Maggie ducked just in time. The ball flew right

round the pole and hit Ella on
the forehead!

Ella made a funny little squeak
and fell flat onto her back. Maggie
tried really hard, but she couldn't
stop herself from giggling.

'ELLA! My poor darling!'
screeched Aunt Celia, as she raced
across the lawn, with Mum and
Dad close behind.

'What have you done, Maggie?'
Aunt Celia asked.

'What?' gasped Maggie.

'It's alright, Mummy,' croaked Ella.
'It doesn't hurt too much. And I'm sure
Maggie didn't mean to hit the ball at
my face.'

'Oh, Maggie,' said Mum, shaking her head.

'But, Mum, it wasn't me!' said Maggie.

'Oh, I suppose poor Ella hit the ball at herself, did she?' snapped Aunt Celia.

'YES! SHE DID!' shouted Maggie.

'That's enough,' said Dad. He was wearing his disappointed face. 'Say sorry to Ella right now.'

Maggie stood with her mouth open in shock. It was SOOOOO UNFAIR!

Finally, she mumbled, 'Sorry.'

'What did you say, Maggie?' asked
Ella. 'I couldn't hear you. My ears are
still ringing from that TERRIBLE
bump on my head.'

'I said SORRY!' shouted Maggie.

'That's alright, Maggie. I forgive
you,' said Ella with a little smile.

Maggie's face felt hot. Her fingers
began to tingle and tiny sparks started
to fizz from her hair.

'I think you'd better take Maggie home,' said Aunt Celia, looking at Maggie nervously.

'Yes, that might be best,' said Mum. 'I'll just say goodbye to Roger–'

'NOW, PLEASE!' screeched Aunt Celia, as more magical sparks began to fill the air around Maggie.

Mum took Maggie's hand and dragged her off to the car. Dad scooped up Alfie and bundled him into his car seat.

The car stayed frostily quiet all the way home.

When they got home, Maggie was sent straight up to bed. She stomped up the stairs and woke up Bat as she slammed her door shut.

Maggie told Bat everything that had happened. 'It was so unfair,' she said. 'I told the truth and nobody believed me. Yet *perfect* Ella told lies and EVERYBODY believed her!

I bet Ella hasn't been sent to bed extra early.'

'You know what, Bat?' said Maggie. 'Telling the truth is overrated. I'm going to try fibbing instead!'

Bat sighed and shook his head.

CHAPTER 2

The next day was a school day.
Maggie woke up, ate her breakfast
and then spent forty-five minutes
drawing up plans for a Bat-sized
jetpack. She was just adding the final
details when Dad called upstairs,
'Have you brushed your teeth, Maggie?'

Oops! Maggie had not brushed
her teeth or combed her hair or
got dressed.

'Um, yes!' lied Maggie, as she quickly pulled on her school uniform.

'Good girl,' said Dad.

'Maggie!' called Mum. 'Have you combed your hair?'

'Yes, Mum,' lied Maggie.

'Good girl,' said Mum.

The doorbell rang and Maggie rushed downstairs.

'That will be Arthur and Charlie,' said Mum, giving Maggie a quick hug. 'Off to school, darling!'

Arthur was Maggie's best friend. He was a smallish boy with big glasses and a worried-looking face. He was wearing a raincoat that was two sizes too big for him and was holding a large carrier bag.

Charlie was Arthur's big brother. He was supposed to walk them to school, but he usually walked a long way behind them with his girlfriend.

Maggie waited until Charlie was far enough back not to hear, then told Arthur her news.

'Arthur,' she said. 'I've decided that from now on I'm going to tell lies, because telling the truth gets you nowhere!'

Arthur was so shocked that he almost dropped his carrier bag. 'You can't do that!' he said.

'I can!' said Maggie. 'It's easy …

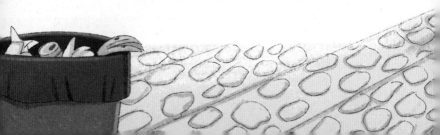

OH, YUCK, ARTHUR! You just trod in DOG POO!'

Arthur looked down in horror … but his shoes were clean.

'You see,' laughed Maggie, 'I'm really good at it!'

Arthur wasn't laughing. 'But Maggie,' he said, 'you *have* to tell the truth. It's *really* important! You can't go around telling lies all the time!'

'Of course, you can't,' said Maggie, putting her hand on Arthur's shoulder. 'Lies work best if you only tell them when you need to!'

When they arrived at school, Maggie finally remembered to ask Arthur what was in his carrier bag.

'My dragon, of course!' he said, proudly pulling out an odd-looking dragon made from cereal boxes,

newspaper and A LOT of glue.
'Where's yours, Maggie?'

Uh-oh! They had all been asked to
make a dragon for their homework.
Their class teacher, Mrs Staples, had
given them ages to do it but Maggie
had forgotten all about it!

'There's only one thing for it …' whispered Maggie, '… a little bit of magic.'

'Oh no,' said Arthur as Maggie reached up her sleeve for her wand. But her wand wasn't there!

'Oh bother! Bat must have hidden it again,' said Maggie.

'You'll just have to tell Mrs Staples that you forgot,' said Arthur. 'I'm sure it will be OK.'

But Maggie wasn't sure at all.

They all trailed into the classroom and sat down on the carpet. One by one, the children took their dragons to the front to show everyone.

Arthur shyly showed everyone his cereal-box masterpiece.

Alma Avukat held up a dragon-like thing made from an old sock.

And Emily Barker presented a dragon with light-up fire and sound effects!

'I bet her mum made that,' whispered Maggie.

Mrs Staples turned to Maggie. 'Maggie, where's your dragon?'

'I couldn't bring it to school,' said Maggie quietly.

'Why not?' asked Mrs Staples.

'Because ... because ...' began Maggie, thinking hard, '... my little brother, Alfie, broke it!'

'Really?' said Mrs Staples.

Maggie nodded. 'He ripped it to pieces! He even ate a bit of its tail!'

Arthur was shocked. His best friend was a FIBBER!

'Couldn't your parents help you to mend it?' asked Mrs Staples.

'No,' said Maggie. 'Because ... Dad was working and Mum ... has, er, a bad arm.'

'Oh dear. How did she hurt her arm?' asked Mrs Staples.

'She fell down the stairs,' Maggie blurted out.

'Oh, Maggie,' said Mrs Staples, 'that's awful! I hope she's better soon. Can you tell us what your dragon looked like?'

'It was brilliant!' said Maggie. 'It was big and red, and it had huge claws and green eyes and lots of teeth!'

'Goodness!' said Mrs Staples. 'Did it have wings?'

'Of course,' said Maggie. 'Big yellow wings that flapped up and down.'

'How long did it take you to make it?' asked Mrs Staples.

'Well,' said Maggie, 'I'm such a good dragon-maker that it only took me one day.' Maggie smiled. She was lying her socks off and it was working!

'That's good to hear, Maggie,' said Mrs Staples.

'Because I'm giving you one more day to make another dragon. You can bring it in tomorrow. I can't wait to see it!'

Oh dear! thought Maggie.

On the walk home, Arthur hardly
said a word to Maggie.

'What's the matter?' Maggie asked.

'You told lies to Mrs Staples.
You said that Alfie ripped up your
dragon,' said Arthur. 'He didn't. You
hadn't even made a dragon!'

'Well, it's the sort of thing that
Alfie would do,' said Maggie as they
reached her house. 'Anyway, see you
tomorrow, Arthur!'

'I'll see you in the classroom,'
said Arthur. 'I don't want to walk to
school with a fibber.'

'I'm not falling for that one again, Maggie!' shouted Arthur. Then …

SQUELCH!

He trod in a dog poo.

CHAPTER 3

'Hello, Maggie! Did you have a
good day at school?' asked Mum.

'Yes, thanks,' said Maggie.
'Mrs Staples said my work
was amazing!'

'That's fantastic! Well done!' said Mum.

Maggie smiled. 'Where's Alfie?' she asked.

'He's upstairs in his cot. Try not to wake him up. I'm trying to finish this bouquet for Mrs Battenberg.'

Maggie tiptoed up to her room.
'Hello, Bat,' she said, bouncing
onto the bed. The little chameleon
clambered up onto her pillow.

'Guess what? I was right about telling lies instead of the truth,' Maggie told him. 'I've been doing it all day and it's brilliant!'

Maggie told Bat all about the lies she'd told and how they had got her out of trouble at school. Bat didn't look impressed. He crossed his arms and slowly shook his head.

But Maggie hardly noticed.
'Now, I just need to make a
fabulous dragon by tomorrow and
everything will be fine,' she said.

Maggie fetched her "making
box" from the wardrobe.

She pulled out cardboard, pipe
cleaners, toilet roll tubes, paint,
glitter and glue, and set to work.

A few minutes later ...

... her dragon was finished.

'What do you think, Bat?' she asked.

Bat took one look at Maggie's masterpiece and burst out laughing.

'Oh, come on, Bat,' said Maggie. 'It's not that bad! Anyway, what is a dragon supposed to look like?'

Bat struck a pose that made him look like a dragon. Maggie looked at Bat. Then she looked at her model dragon again. 'Mine looks more like a robot pig with wonky wings, doesn't it?'

Bat nodded.

'Oh, this is hopeless!' cried Maggie, angrily tearing her dragon into little pieces. 'Why couldn't my dragon look more like you, Bat? You'd make a brilliant dragon.'

Suddenly, Maggie had a fantastic idea!

If she could stick some wings on Bat, get him to turn red and sprinkle him with glitter, she could take him to school and pretend she'd made him.

All she needed was a little bit of MAGIC!

Bat covered his eyes. Maggie snatched up her wand, gave it a wiggle and chanted:

'Little Bat with shaking knees, turn into a dragon, please!'

POOF!

A small puff of smoke surrounded Bat, who was now bright red, very glittery and had an impressive pair of wings.

Maggie was thrilled. Bat was not.

The glitter was itchy and the wings felt weird. Bat flapped and flapped, trying to shake them off, but all the flapping made him fly! He whizzed around the bedroom, bumped his head on the ceiling, bounced off the wardrobe, knocked all the books out of the bookcase and landed with a FLUMP on Maggie's bed.

'Are you OK, Bat?' asked Maggie.

Bat opened his mouth and out came a little jet of fire!

'Oh dear!' said Maggie. She ran to open the window to let out the smoke. 'I was hoping you'd look a bit more ... cardboardy. You weren't supposed to be a REAL DRAGON!'

'Maggie?' called Mum. 'What's going on up there?'

Maggie opened her bedroom door, rushed over to the stairs and called down, 'Nothing bad! I am just making a dragon for my school project.'

Mum didn't look convinced.

Then three things happened all at once:

1. Bat (the dragon) flew straight out of the window!

2. Alfie (who had just learnt how to climb out of his cot) crawled into Maggie's bedroom without her noticing.

3. Mum started walking up the stairs.

I'm in so much trouble, thought Maggie.

Mum pushed open Maggie's bedroom door and gasped in horror.

CHAPTER 4

Maggie's bedroom was a mess and sitting in the middle of it was Alfie, surrounded by torn up pieces of cardboard dragon.

'ALFIE!' cried Mum.

'Alfie?' said Maggie.

'Oh, Maggie,' said Mum. 'I'm so sorry.'

'You're sorry?' said Maggie.

'Yes,' said Mum. 'Look! Alfie's torn your homework to pieces.'

'Oh no,' said Maggie, but she was thinking, *Oh yes!* 'It doesn't matter,

Mum. He's only little, and it wasn't a very good dragon.'

'That's very kind of you, Maggie, but that's not the point. That was very naughty, Alfie. You must not break Maggie's things!'

Mum scooped Alfie up and took him downstairs.

Alfie was NOT impressed.

Maggie felt a little bit guilty, but she hadn't even lied! She just hadn't told the truth. It wasn't *her* fault that Mum blamed Alfie. Was it?

'Did you see that, Bat?' Maggie asked.

But Bat wasn't there.

At that moment, Bat was flying
through the park, trying to keep close
to the trees so nobody could see him.
It didn't work very well. He kept
bumping into the branches, scattering
birds and squirrels in all directions.

Flying was hard work. Bat was
very tired, but he bravely kept going —
through the park and into the woods
until, at last, he saw a small cottage.

He tried to land neatly by the front door, but flew straight into it instead.

A few seconds later, the door creaked open. Bat saw a jolly, whiskery old man looking down at him. It was Grandad Sparks.

'Hello, Bat,' he said. 'Goodness, you're looking rather more DRAGONY than usual.'

Grandad Sparks took Bat inside and sat him on the sofa. Then he searched through a shelf full of potion ingredients. He poured out a bowl of sundried flies (Bat's favourite) and sprinkled them

with a pinch of his newly-invented
"Back to Normal" powder.

By the time Bat had finished his
snack, apart from the odd smoky
hiccup, he was a chameleon again.

'Let's get you home,' said Grandad

Sparks, popping Bat into his coat pocket. Then he took out his wand, gave it a little wave and chanted:

'Eye of newt and
leg of toad.
Off to Number One
Park Road!'

POOF!

They were suddenly standing on the doorstep of Maggie's house. Grandad Sparks rang the doorbell.

'Oh, hello,' said Mum, as she opened the door with Alfie perched

on her hip. 'This is a nice surprise.
Come in!'

Grandad Sparks kissed Mum on
the cheek, then tickled Alfie into
fits of giggles.

'Where's Maggie?' asked
Grandad Sparks.

'She's upstairs, trying to make another dragon for her school project,' said Mum.

'Another one?' said Grandad Sparks.

'Alfie destroyed the first one,' said Mum.

'Did he?' said Grandad Sparks.

Mum nodded. Alfie shook his head.

'Perhaps I can help her with her dragon?' said Grandad Sparks.

'That would be lovely!' said Mum.

'GRANDAD!' shouted Maggie as he peeped through her door.

She ran over and hugged him.
'What are you doing here?'
'Well,' said Grandad Sparks,
'I had an unexpected visitor
and I thought you'd
like to see him.'

He reached into his pocket and pulled out ... 'Bat!' cried Maggie. 'Thank goodness! Are you alright?'

Bat nodded and then went off for a rest on his sleeping stick.

'Now then, Maggie Moo,' said Grandad. 'I think you'd better tell me what's been going on.'

'I had to make a dragon for my school project,' said Maggie, 'and I did but ... but ... Alfie tore it up.'

'Did he?' asked Grandad Sparks.

'Um ... yes,' said Maggie, looking down at the floor. It felt awful to lie to Grandad Sparks. 'I tried to use magic because Mrs Staples only gave

me one day to make another dragon,
which isn't very long. But my magic
went a bit wrong. I accidentally turned
Bat into a real dragon and he flew out
of the window.'

'Anything else?' asked Grandad Sparks.

'Arthur doesn't like me anymore,' said Maggie, sadly.

'Really, why?' asked Grandad Sparks.

Maggie really wanted to tell Grandad Sparks the truth.

But then she would have to tell him about all the lies she'd told. And maybe *he* wouldn't like her anymore either! So she lied again.

'I think it was something about a dog poo,' she said.

'Don't worry. I'm sure you'll find a way to be friends again,' said Grandad Sparks. 'But, for now, shall I help you make a new dragon?'

'Yes, please!' said Maggie.

'OK,' said Grandad Sparks, taking out his wand. 'Put all the torn-up pieces in a pile and stand back.'

Then he waved his wand and
chanted:

'With magic smoke
and mystic vapour,
come forth a dragon
made of paper!'

POOF!

A dragon appeared. It was made
of paper and paint, with cardboard
wings that flapped up and down
when you pulled its tail.

'It's perfect!' said Maggie.

'You haven't seen the best bit yet,'
said Grandad Sparks. 'Look into
its eyes.'

Maggie stared into the dragon's
eyes. They glowed bright green!

'WOW!' she said. 'That's magical!'
(which was absolutely true).

CHAPTER 5

The next day, Maggie woke up early. She couldn't wait to show everyone her dragon! She ran downstairs with it clutched under her arm.

'Have you brushed your teeth, Maggie?' asked Dad.

Maggie tried to say, 'Yes, Dad!' (which was a lie). But what came out her mouth was, 'No, I couldn't be bothered!' (which was the truth).

'Well, go back upstairs and brush them,' said Dad.

'Have you combed your hair, Maggie?' asked Mum.

Maggie tried to say, 'Yes, Mum!' (which was a lie). But what came out of her mouth was, 'No, I didn't feel like it!' (which was the truth).

So Mum sent Maggie off to fetch the comb and combed it for her.

DING DONG!

'That'll be Grandad!' cried Maggie as she ran towards the door.

But it wasn't Grandad, it was Penny the postwoman. She gave Mum a small brown parcel. Inside was a box of chocolates with a note.

Sorry to hear about your tumble. I hope these will make you feel better!
Best wishes,
Mrs Staples

'Why has Mrs Staples sent me chocolates?' asked Mum. 'What does she mean about a "tumble"?'

Maggie wanted to say, 'I don't know,' (which was a lie). But she could feel the truth bouncing around inside her head, trying to get out. She put both hands over her mouth to stop it, but it was no use!

'Well, actually,' she started, then–

DING DONG!

The doorbell rang again and Mum rushed to answer it before Maggie could finish her sentence.

Phew!

It was Grandad Sparks, ready to walk Maggie to school.

'Hi, Grandad! Bye, Mum. Bye, Dad. Bye, Alfie,' Maggie called, as she ran out of the house, stuffing her dragon into her bag.

Maggie kept a lookout for Arthur on the way to school, but she didn't see him anywhere.

In the classroom, Mrs Staples sat everyone on the carpet and took the register. Then she turned to Maggie and said, 'Have you got something to show us this morning?'

'Yes,' said Maggie and took the dragon out of her bag.

Everyone went 'Oooh' and 'Aah' as Maggie showed them how it flapped its wings.

'Oh, Maggie, it's wonderful!' said Mrs Staples. 'Is this dragon the same as the one Alfie destroyed?'

Maggie tried to say, 'Yes,' (which was a lie). But what came out of her mouth was, 'Alfie didn't tear my dragon up. I just said that because I'd forgotten to make one.'

Everyone was shocked. Especially Maggie!

Now she'd started telling the truth, she just couldn't stop! 'My mum didn't fall down the stairs and hurt her arm,' she said. 'But she did really like the chocolates you sent her. And I did try to make a dragon, but it looked like a robot pig with wings, so I tore it up.'

'I see,' said Mrs Staples. But Maggie hadn't finished.

'Then Mum thought Alfie had torn it up and I didn't tell her it was me,' she said.

'Oh, Maggie,' said Mrs Staples, shaking her head. 'Did you make this dragon all by yourself?'

'No,' said Maggie, miserably. 'I collected all the pieces of my old dragon and my Grandad made them into this dragon. He's a wizard ...'

Arthur jumped up. 'Yes, he's a-a

wizard at making models!' he said quickly. He couldn't let Maggie tell everyone the secret about her family's magic. She would be in SO much trouble.

'Thank you, Arthur,' said Mrs Staples. 'Sit down, please.'

Maggie's face felt very hot. She felt embarrassed but strangely calm, as though a big weight had been lifted off her shoulders.

Mrs Staples asked Miss Turner to keep an eye on the class. Then she took Maggie to the quiet room.

'Why have you been telling so many lies, Maggie?' asked Mrs Staples.

Maggie didn't even want to lie now. She told Mrs Staples the whole truth. 'I lied because nobody believed me when I told the truth

about Ella's bump on the head.
I told the truth and I got told off.
But Ella lied and everyone believed
her. So then I decided to lie too.'

'And how did lying make you feel, Maggie?' asked Mrs Staples.

'Well, it was OK to start with, but then it made me feel bad. The more lies I told, the harder it was to tell the truth. And now everyone will hate me!'

'No, they won't,' said Mrs Staples. 'You've done the right thing now, by telling the truth. Trust me, Maggie, it will be fine.'

And it was! Nobody in class made her feel bad, and best of all, Arthur was her friend again. He even shared his jam tart with her at lunchtime.

Grandad Sparks picked Maggie up from school. He chatted to Arthur's mum while Arthur and Maggie walked ahead.

'Thanks for helping me in class, Arthur,' said Maggie. 'I nearly told everyone about Grandad Sparks being a wizard!'

'That's OK,' said Arthur. 'I didn't think you'd want everyone to know. Why did you tell the truth about, well, everything?' asked Arthur.

'I couldn't help it!' said Maggie. 'When I looked into the eyes of my dragon, all the truths came spilling out!'

106

'Magic, I expect,' said Arthur.

'Grandad Sparks's magic, I expect,'
said Maggie looking back at
her Grandad.

'I'm glad you're not a
fibber anymore,' said Arthur.

'Me too,' said Maggie,

as they reached her front door. 'See you tomorrow!'

Maggie and Grandad Sparks stepped into the house.

There was a strange smell coming from the kitchen. Grandad Sparks took one sniff, whispered 'Bye, Maggie!' and disappeared.

Dad popped his head round the door and said, 'Hi, Maggie. Mum's had to deliver that bouquet, so I'm making dinner tonight. It's a new recipe, come and have a taste.'

Dad handed Maggie a spoonful of gloopy brown mixture. She took a tiny mouthful.

'How does it taste?' Dad asked.
'YUCKY!' said Maggie.
'Yucky?' said Dad. 'You could have
at least pretended to like it.'

'But that would have been telling a lie,' said Maggie, smiling. 'And isn't it always better to tell the truth?'

Dad chuckled. 'Yes, it is. Would you like pizza instead?'

'YES! I really would!' said Maggie (which was absolutely true).

Continue the magic in ...

MAGGIE SPARKS

AND THE
SCHOOL OF
SLIME